A PROM TO REMEMBER

Adapted by Sarah Nathan

Based on the screenplay written by Peter Barsocchini

Based on characters created by Peter Barsocchini

Executive Producer Kenny Ortega

Produced by Bill Borden and Barry Rosenbush

Directed by Kenny Ortega

Copyright © 2008 Disney Enterprises, Inc.

All rights reserved. Published by Disney Press, an imprint of Disney Book Group. No part of this book may be reproduced or transmitted in any form or by any means, electronic or mechanical, including photocopying, recording, or by any information storage and retrieval system, without written permission from the publisher.

For information address Disney Press, 114 Fifth Avenue, New York, New York 10011-5690.

Printed in the United States of America

First Edition

1 3 5 7 9 10 8 6 4 2

Library of Congress Control Number: 2008904378

ISBN 978-1-4231-1205-1

For more Disney Press fun, visit www.disneybooks.com

Visit DisneyChannel.com/HighSchoolMusical

NEW YORK

The Wildcats basketball team had done it again. They won the championship game against their rivals, West High! After the game, everyone headed back to Troy Bolton's house to celebrate. He and Gabriella Montez took a break from the party and talked in his tree house.

Now that the championship game was over, Troy could focus on other things, such as asking Gabriella to the senior prom. He wanted to find the perfect way to invite her.

Troy took Gabriella to the rooftop garden at school, where they had had many private talks. He reached into his pocket and took out two tickets to the East High senior prom, the Last Waltz.

Gabriella was thrilled. Meeting Troy and having so many new friends had made her senior year a dream come true. Together, she and Troy twirled and waltzed around the garden until a light rain sprinkled down on them.

"Is that a yes?" Troy asked, realizing that Gabriella had not agreed to be his date yet.

Gabriella smiled. "In every language," she replied.

Gabriella and Troy weren't the only seniors at East High thinking about the prom. Zeke Baylor had been planning to ask Sharpay Evans all year. He finally got up the courage to invite her and headed to Sharpay's dressing room.

"Sharpay," he began nervously. "There's something I've been wanting to ask you for about a year, and I really . . ."

But Sharpay didn't give him a chance to finish his sentence.

"Oh, Zeke, glad you stopped by. You're taking me to prom," she told him. "Don't buy a corsage, it's being flown in from Hawaii."

Zeke was shocked, and even more so when Sharpay mentioned dance lessons! "Beginning Monday. Questions? No? Good. Toodles," she said, closing the door. Zeke stood dumbfounded. He couldn't believe that Sharpay had said yes!

Taylor McKessie was waiting for Chad Danforth to ask her to the prom. With Troy's help, Chad was hoping that his lunchtime surprise would win Taylor over. Swapping the basketball in his hand for some fresh-cut flowers, he went over to where Taylor was sitting in the cafeteria. Troy raised his arms, and everyone in the room became silent. "Taylor McKessie," Chad announced, "please be my date for the senior prom?"

Taylor smiled. "I'd be honored," she replied. The students in the cafeteria cheered loudly.

Later that week, while working on the yearbook after school, Gabriella told Taylor a big secret. She had been accepted into the freshman honors program at Stanford University—and it started in a couple of weeks!

Gabriella wasn't sure if she was going to attend. She didn't know what to do. How could she say good-bye to Troy? Would she come back for the prom? And what about starring in the senior musical that Kelsi Nielsen was writing?

Meanwhile, Kelsi was working hard on writing songs for the senior musical. She was thinking of little else but music. Little did she know that Sharpay was watching her closely. Sharpay didn't want her to write the best song in the show for Gabriella and Troy because *she* wanted the spotlight. She told her brother, Ryan, to spy on Kelsi to see what kinds of songs she was composing.

Gabriella was torn, but she decided to attend the freshman honors program. Saying good-bye was very hard. After she left, everyone missed her, but Troy missed her most of all. Nothing was the same. The senior musical rehearsals, the rooftop garden, and even the cafeteria, were difficult to be in without her. Everything reminded him of Gabriella.

Being away from Troy and the rest of the Wildcats was harder for Gabriella than she had thought it would be. The idea of going back for the prom and graduation was too much for her to imagine. It was difficult enough to leave Troy once. She didn't want to have to say good-bye again. Two days before the prom, she called Troy and tearfully confessed to him on the phone. "I think I've run out of good-byes," she said sadly. "I need to stay right where I am."

Troy thought about the choices he was about to face in his own life. He told his dad about his plans for college. He didn't want to just play basketball—he also wanted to act.

Gabriella had shown him how exciting it was to be onstage, and he loved it. Maybe the University of Albuquerque wasn't the only place for him. Ms. Darbus had told him to trust his instincts. And he was going to. That night he made his decision about the prom . . . *and* his future.

The rest of the Wildcats were anxiously preparing for their senior prom. There were dresses to be bought, tuxedos to rent, corsages to order—the halls of East High were buzzing with excitement! The seniors couldn't wait for the magical night, *especially* Sharpay.

The senior prom had finally arrived! The gymnasium had been transformed into a magical ballroom. Everyone looked their best—the girls in fancy gowns and the boys in tuxedos. It was going to be an amazing night!

As the Wildcats entered the room, they couldn't wait to hit the dance floor! Kelsi and Ryan twirled each other around; Taylor and Chad tried to outdo each other's dance moves; and Martha taught Jason some new hip-hop steps. Sharpay was very pleased at how Zeke's dance lessons had transformed him into a dazzling ballroom dancer.

The prom was everything the East High seniors had hoped it would be. The music was spectacular, the decorations were perfect, and the dance floor was packed with students. But even though the Wildcats were having a great time, they all thought that the evening would have been absolutely perfect if only Troy and Gabriella were there with them.

At Stanford, Gabriella strolled back to her dorm room through the quad. Suddenly, she spotted Troy's truck in the parking lot.

"Figured you'd be the last one out of the building," Troy commented from his perch high up in a tree.

Gabriella looked up and saw that Troy was dressed in his tuxedo. "I took a wrong turn on the way to my prom," he told her, giving her a wide smile.

Gabriella couldn't believe that Troy had traveled so far to see her. "But prom is tonight . . ." she told him. "In Albuquerque. And that's a thousand miles away."

"My prom is wherever you are," he said earnestly and climbed down from the tree. Troy held out his hand, and together they walked around the quad.

As they twirled around the fountain in the glowing sunset, Gabriella and Troy imagined that they were dancing with their friends at the East High prom. They were able to enjoy the thrill of being there—and most importantly—being together. It was a night that Gabriella and Troy would never forget.

When their waltz ended, Gabriella and Troy took a walk and watched a beautiful sunset. "It's the best prom I could have imagined, Troy," Gabriella said. Troy looked into her eyes and smiled.

Just then, Troy grabbed Gabriella's hands. Gabriella had made him think differently about things, and people.

"Kids I used to pass in the hallway, we're all friends now," he said. "East High changed when you got there," Troy told her, remembering how different things were before Gabriella arrived. "And now it's changed because you left."

Gabriella began to wonder if she should go back to see her friends. She thought of how hard Kelsi had worked on the musical and how she would love to hang out with the rest of the Wildcats again. "You may be ready to say good-bye to East High, but East High isn't ready to say good-bye to you," Troy said.

Gabriella knew what she had to do. She was definitely going back to East High to join her friends for the senior musical and graduation. But for now, she was going to treasure the moment— and make her prom last as long as possible.

Gabriella had never felt happier. With the Wildcats by your side, she thought to herself, dreams really can come true. And for her and Troy, and all of the Wildcats, the senior prom was a night they'd remember forever.